E
ELK   copy 1
            ELKIN, BENJAMIN

E   AUTHOR
ELK   SIX FOOLISH FISHERMEN

          TITLE

DATE DUE

FAC 8			
Fac K			

Invitations to Personal Reading
Curriculum Foundation Classroom Library
Scott, Foresman and Company

Books to Read Aloud

The Big Golden Book of Poetry	edited by Jane Werner
Finders Keepers	Will and Nicolas
Little Frightened Tiger	Golden MacDonald
The Man Who Didn't Wash His Dishes	Phyllis Krasilovsky
The Old Woman and Her Pig	illustrated by Paul Galdone
Rosa-Too-Little	Sue Felt
Six Foolish Fishermen	retold by Benjamin Elkin
The Three Billy Goats Gruff	P. C. Asbjørnsen and J. E. Moe
Umbrella	Taro Yashima
Where Does the Butterfly Go When It Rains	May Garelick

Books to Enrich the Content Fields

The Big Book of Real Fire Engines	illustrated by George Zaffo
The Listening Walk	Paul Showers
One Snail and Me	Emilie McLeod
The Sky Was Blue	Charlotte Zolotow
What Is A Turtle	Gene Darby

Books for Independent Reading

Belling the Cat and Other Stories	retold by Leland Jacobs
Big Talk	Miriam Schlein
Cowboy Small	Lois Lenski
Gertie the Duck	Nicholas Georgiady and Louis Romano
Indian Two Feet and His Horse	Margaret Friskey
Josie and the Snow	Helen Buckley
Karen's Opposites	A. and M. Provensen
Millions and Millions and Millions!	Louis Slobodkin
Nothing but Cats, Cats, Cats	Grace Skaar
Robins and Rabbits	John Hawkinson

Six
Foolish Fishermen

Based on a folktale in Ashton's

Chap-books of the Eighteenth Century, 1882

By BENJAMIN ELKIN

Illustrations by Katherine Evans

CHILDRENS PRESS

Special Scott, Foresman and Company Edition
for the *Invitations to Personal Reading* Program

This edition is printed and distributed by
Scott, Foresman and Company by special
arrangement with Childrens Press,
1224 West Van Buren Street,
Chicago, Illinois 60607.

Once there were six brothers
who decided to go
fishing. So they
went to the river
and picked good spots
from which to fish.

"I will sit in this boat,"
said the first brother.

"And I will kneel on this raft,"
said the second brother.

"And I will lean on this log,"
said the third brother.

"And I will stand on this
bridge," said the fourth brother.

"And I will lie on this rock,"
said the fifth brother.

"And I will walk on this bank,"
said the sixth brother.

And that is exactly what they did.
Each brother fished from the
spot he had chosen, and each one
had good luck.

But when it was time to go home,
the brothers became a little
worried.

"We have been near the river,
and over the river, and on the
river," said the brother in
the boat. "One of us might
easily have fallen into the water
and been drowned. I shall count
all the brothers to be sure there
are six of us."
And he began to count:

"I see one
brother on the raft,
That's *one*.

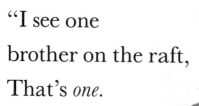

And another
on the log.
That's *two*.

And another
on the bridge.
That's *three*.

And another
on the rock.
That's *four*.

And another
on the bank.
That's *five*.

"Only *five!* Woe is me. We have
lost a brother!" In his sorrow he
didn't even notice that he had
forgotten to count himself.

"Can it really be?" cried the brother on the raft. "Has one of us been drowned, and have we really lost a brother?"

And he, too, began to count:

St. James School
1215 B STREET
DAVIS, CALIF. 95616

"I see one
brother on
the log.
That's *one*.

And another
on the bridge.
That's *two*.

And another
on the rock.
That's *three*.

And another
on the bank.
That's *four*.

And another
in the boat.
That's *five*.

"Only *five*. What will our dear
mother say?"

And he, too, didn't even notice
that he had forgotten to count
himself.

"Let me check from here!"
cried the brother
on the log.

"I see one brother on the bridge. That's *one*.

"And another on the rock. That's *two*.

"And another on the bank. That's *three*.

"And another in the boat.
That's *four*.

"And another on the raft.
That's *five*. *Five* in *all*,
oh, unhappy day! Why did
we ever come here, for one
of us to be drowned!"

Then the fourth brother
counted, and the fifth and
the sixth—each one counted
only five brothers because
each forgot to include himself.

All the brothers went back
to the shore and rushed sadly
up and down the river's edge,
trying to see the body of
their poor drowned brother.

Then along came a boy who
had also been fishing, but who
had not caught a single fish.

"What's the matter?" he asked.
"You seem to have plenty of
fish. Why do you all look so sad?"

"Because six of us came here to
fish, and now there are only five
of us left. One of our dear
brothers has been drowned!"

The boy looked puzzled. "What
do you mean, only five left?
How do you figure that?"

"Look, I'll show you," said
the eldest brother, and he
pointed to his brothers:
"One.
     Two.
          Three.
               Four.
                    Five.

"Six of us came here, and now
only five are going back. Sad
is the day!"
The boy turned to hide his smile,
and then he turned back. "I think
I can help you find your lost
brother," he said. "When I squeeze
your hand, I want you to count."

As hard as he could, he squeezed
the hand of each of the brothers,
in turn.

"*One!*" yelled the first brother,
and he rubbed his aching hand.

"*Two!*" cried the second brother,
and he jumped up and down because
of the hard squeeze.

"*Three!*" shouted the third brother.

"*Four!*" shrieked the fourth brother.

"*Five!*" screamed the fifth brother.

"*Six!*" roared the sixth brother.

SIX! The brothers looked at
each other in delight.

There were six of them again!
They cheered for joy, and
slapped each other on the back.

Gratefully, they turned to the
boy. "Here," they said, "We
insist that you take all of our
fish. We can never thank you
enough for finding our dear,
lost brother."

As the boy happily accepted
their gift, the six foolish
fisherman went their merry way.